Time for a Swim

written by Pam Holden
illustrated by Lamia Aziz

We went to the river
to have a swim.
"I swim here," said Hippo.

"I swim in this river, too," said Turtle.
We didn't swim there!

We went to have a swim in the sea.
"I swim here," said Octopus.

"I swim in the sea, too,"
said Dolphin.
We didn't swim there!

We went to the lake to have a swim.
"I swim here," said Beaver.

"I swim on this lake, too," said Swan.
We didn't swim there!

We went to have a
swim at the beach.
"I swim here," said Fish.

"I swim at this beach, too," said Crab.
We didn't swim there!

We went to the stream
to have a swim.
"I swim here," said Duck.

"I swim in this stream, too," said Eel.
We didn't swim there!

We went to have a swim in the pond.
"I swim here," said Frog.

"I swim on this pond, too," said Goose.
We didn't swim there!

We went to the pool
to have a swim.
"I swim in this pool,"
said the boy.

"I swim here, too,"
said the girl.
"Come in for a swim
in the pool."

We had a swim in the pool.
It was cool.
Splash!